P9-BBV-967

For my daughters —M.W.L.

For Zachary —A.H.

THIS IS A BORZOI BOOK PUBLISHED BY ALFRED A. KNOPF

Visit us on the Web! randomhousekids.com

Educators and librarians, for a variety of teaching tools, visit us at RHTeachersLibrarians.com

Library of Congress Cataloging-in-Publication Data
Names: Lloyd, Megan Wagner, author. | Halpin, Abigail, illustrator.
Title: Fort-building time / Megan Wagner Lloyd ; illustrated by Abigail Halpin.
Description: First edition. | New York : Alfred A. Knopf, 2017. | Summary: "An exploration of building forts throughout all four seasons." —Provided by publisher | Description based on print version record and CIP data provided by publisher; resource not viewed.
Identifiers: LCCN 2016025703 (print) | LCCN 2016004625 (ebook) | ISBN 978-0-399-55655-5 (trade) | ISBN 978-0-399-55656-2 (lib. bdg.) | ISBN 978-0-399-55657-9 (ebook)
Subjects: | CYAC: Building—Fiction. | Seasons—Fiction.
Classification: LCC PZ7.1.L59 (print) | LCC PZ7.1.L59 Fo 2017 (ebook) | DDC [E]—dc23

The illustrations in this book were created using watercolor and colored pencil, and finished digitally.

MANUFACTURED IN CHINA
October 2017
10 9 8 7 6 5 4

First Edition

FORT-BUILDING TIME

BY MEGAN WAGNER LLOYD

PICTURES BY

ABIGAIL HALPIN

Alfred A. Knopf New York

WINTER

is a snowball-throwing, scarf-wrapping, sled-pulling, ice-sliding time.

A dog-snuggling, cocoa-drinking,
snowman-making, fort-building time!

SPRING

is a daffodil-hunting, umbrella-holding,
rain-watching, mud-squishing time.

A rainbow-finding, spaceship-drawing,
book-reading, fort-building time!

SUMMER

is a wave-racing, sun-sizzling,
saltwater-swimming, picnic-eating time.

A sandcastle-shaping, crab-digging,
shell-stacking, fort-building time!

FALL

is a leaf-chasing, wind-rocking
poem-writing, soup-sipping tim

A sword-fighting, trail-climbing,
woods-exploring, fort-building time!

Every season has its own secret-dreaming,

cozy-keeping, hush-listening, fort-building time.

So let's make today a

box-taping, clothespin-clipping—

OH NO!

Everything-slipping...

fort-FALLING time!

A project-fixing, secret entrance-crawling, spyglass-peering, fort-building time!